BIG MONTY

and THE LUNATIC LUNCH LADY

BY

MATT MAXX

BIG MONTY AND THE LUNATIC LUNCH LADY

Printed in the United States of America
First Printing, 2019

ISBN: 978-1-7337435-0-1

Dedication
To all the kids out there
just trying to be themselves.
~ Matt Maxx

Table of Contents

CHAPTER 1

5th Grade Homies and One Dumb Name

I was chillin' at my locker, minding my own when Antavius LaRoyce Jenkins, AKA A'lo, slid up next to me wearing busted up Jordans. I looked down at his two-foot-tall self and couldn't for the life of me understand why everybody at Washington Carver Elementary was so scared of this chump.

Maybe it's that lopsided haircut his brother in barber school gives him. Maybe it's that fake grill he wears on weekends. I'm willing to bet it's because he tells "Yo' Mama" jokes better than any kid in the fifth grade.

"Hey Bruh, lemme get a dollar for some ice cream," A'lo said. He reached around me and slammed my friend Global's locker door shut just as he was trying to pull out his backpack. Global doesn't bother anyone. Jordy Jones is his real name, but everyone calls him Global. That kid is so smart there is nothing on earth he doesn't know.

Global gave up trying to pull his backpack out of the jammed locker door. As he turned to head down the hall carrying all his stuff in his arms, A'lo lifted his dusty hands and smacked Global's books on the floor. Man! That A'lo is so disrespectful.

Global scooped his books together and took off. "I keep stacks of cash, Bro, but you can't be asking every day," I told A'lo.

"I keep stacks of cash . . . Bro!" A'lo mimicked me in a whiny voice, blowing his bad breath in my face. "Bruh, you sound goofy! Stop playing. You wouldn't know a stack if it slapped you in your face."

"I got a boatload of stacks," I said.

"Man, quit trippin'. With a name like Merlin, all you got is boatloads of nerd friends. Just gimme some money for ice cream."

That's right, my name is Merlin. Merlin Montgomery. My parents, who say they were the coolest couple on the block, somehow decided to name their firstborn son Merlin.

Tell me about it. And you thought you had problems? I'm probably the only kid named Merlin in my town. No, make that my state. No, the entire country. Let's face it, probably the whole world. Nobody's named their kid Merlin since before the first black president, or maybe even longer.

I asked my mom was she drinking too much diet soda with the bad chemicals in it while she was pregnant with me. I asked my dad was he inhaling too many fumes at his summer job painting swimming pools.

They both said, "No!" They were "enlightened." By enlightened, they meant they read a bunch of books by famous people, got good grades, and knew enough to put their napkins in their laps at dinner.

My parents met at Fisk University in Nashville as biology majors. My dad said, "We named you after the most famous wizard of all time because your mom and I made magic when we made you." Yuck! Can you even?

"Merlin" might be the only thing my parents ever agreed on. I don't even remember them as a couple, but unlucky for me, they made it long enough to come up with one dumb name.

I handed A'Lo money for his ice cream, but only because I had a Mega-Blastoise Pokémon card I wanted to trade with Global before lunch. Plus, for some reason, all the cool kids liked A'lo. And hey, I'm down with them, too.

"A'lo, I told you a million times," I called after him as he ran down the hall, "call me Big Monty!"

CHAPTER 2

Taco Tuesday and One Loony Lunch Lady

"Global, hold up! Wait for me." I caught up with the Pokémon crew just in time to trade two Meg cards for a valuable Mewtwo Full Art card while we waited in line for Taco Tuesday.

Taco Tuesdays are the only school lunch worth waiting for. I grabbed my tray, still damp and slimy from kids in the first lunch period, and moved down the line. My thumb stuck in some kind of dried yellow crusty thing plastered to the corner of the tray. "Yuck! What is that!?" Probably nasty gravy leftover from Meatloaf Monday.

Ms. Freddy, a lady who has worked in the cafeteria since my dad was a kid, yelled at us to move on down.

"Hey, Ms. Freddy!" I called in my loud voice.

"Hey there, Ruby!"

Ruby? Ruby was a girl in my class with long braids and cowgirl boots. How in the world did Ms. Freddy think I looked like

Ruby? Man was I glad A'Lo wasn't there to hear that. I grabbed my strawberry milk and moved down the line toward the meanest lunch lady in the whole wide world.

Mrs. Findlehorner was waiting there holding a metal spoon like a Katana sword, glaring down at me with eyes like lasers. Did you know laser is actually an acronym? An acronym is an abbreviation formed from the initial letters of other words and pronounced as a word. Acronyms are like nicknames made up of the first letter of each word—like NASA or YOLO. Can you guess what "laser" really stands for? See the end of this chapter and I'll fill you in.

Back to lunch. Findlehorner's greasy hair was slicked back so tight it looked like her eyes might bulge out of her head. She tightened her plastic gloves. Snap! All of a sudden, I realized those weren't tacos in her tray. It was leftover Monday Meatloaf.

Disgusting!

Meatloaf Monday is bad enough once a week, but twice? That's uncalled for. She scooped up that gray piece of meat in her slotted spoon. Gravy hung down like snot on a preschool kid's face. She slapped that slop on my plate and glared at me like she was daring me to say something. And I did.

"What happened to Taco Tuesday?"

Mrs. Findlehorner slammed her metal spoon down on the stand and flared her nostrils. Her nose holes moved in and out while she blew her huffy breath all over that nasty meat. "You kids are too good for leftovers?"

I don't know what came over me. I blurted out, "No offense, but it isn't leftovers if it wasn't food to begin with."

Ms. Findlehorner's eyes narrowed. She squinted at me like she was going to jump over that cafeteria counter and pound me into some meatloaf.

Global pushed me in the back, "Merlin, I mean, Big Monty, you better move."

I'm about to nerd-out on y'all. You ready? Yo, don't worry, nobody's listening. Remember, it's nerds who rule the world!

Laser—like the light beams you see shooting out of spaceships in movies—is actually an acronym for "Light Amplification by Stimulated Emission of Radiation." Let's break that down.

We all know what light is, but an "amplified light" means that it is being made stronger—like a superpower light.

But a laser's light is made stronger by something. It is "stimulated" by something. Stimulated means activated, or kicked in the butt to get going. Like when your mama yells

at you to get out of bed so you don't miss the bus.

So light is stimulated, or kicked in the butt, by an "emission of radiation." Emission means to send out. It's like emitting smells when you force out a big one. And radiation— well, that's a whole other lesson. Just think of your microwave. Let's just say radiation is energy in the form of invisible waves.

Now read it again and see if you've got it straight. Laser is really an acronym for "Light Amplification by Stimulated Emission of Radiation." See? I knew you were smarter than you looked! Dude, I'm only joking. You know I can't actually see you, right?

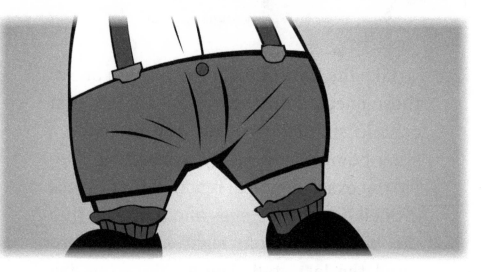

CHAPTER 3

Brown Grapes and One Busted Merlin

I scanned the cafeteria. Since Global and I were in the same class, it wouldn't seem too suspect if I sat next to him at lunch. I like the dude, but Global wears the same pants he wore in second grade that were probably too short even back then. He also sports brown socks, but the kid is mad-smart and wicked funny.

Like the time Global messed with one of those cheap dollar store shaving kits that contain sulfur hydroxide, and he made a stink bomb that actually worked. He copied the exact chemical reaction that causes a smell like rotting eggs and lobbed it into the boys' bathroom right after A'lo entered the last stall. The smell of ten-day old moose vomit filled the hallways. Kids in line started retching, and some kids got sick enough to go home early. It was so bad everybody called A'lo "The Lock Mess Monster" for the rest of the year. Behind his back of course. Nobody but me knew Global was behind that whole prank.

We sat down. I pushed my tray forward. Even the fruit salad looked slimy and sad today. While Global devoured his meal, I settled for my strawberry milk. It was better than nothing.

"How can you eat that slop?" I asked him.

"It has no taste. I tell myself it is a sponge with nutritional value." Nutritional value means the food has vitamins in it, and it's good for you, but that is hard to believe.

Just as I decided to try the mashed potatoes that looked like old Elmer's glue, I felt it. Something warm, wet, and squishy hit me on the back of the neck. Slap! It started to slide down toward my collar.

"What the…?" I knew what it was before I reached back and touched it because I heard A'Lo and his buddies laughing. That little punk threw his meatloaf at me!

That was it. I'd had enough of A'lo for one day. I couldn't let this loud mouth and his buddies front on me like that. I filled my plastic spoon with two browning grapes and a raisin and aimed it right at his crooked hairline. Thwack! It stuck straight to that lopsided flat top and hung on. Now, I was laughing with A'lo's buddies, instead. I laughed so hard I shot the last of my strawberry milk right out my nose!

"Look at that fool!" I snorted at Global. A'lo tried to wipe the rotting fruit out of his hair with those cheap little school lunch napkins. The napkins kept breaking up and sticking all in his hair like miniature rock climbers.

Global wasn't laughing. I turned around to help him find a sense of humor, but standing right behind me was none other than Mrs. Findlerhorner!

"Busted." She said with flecks of spit flying out of her mouth. They landed over me. She grabbed my collar, twisted me up off the lunchroom bench, and dragged my skinny bones down the hall to the principal's office.

On the way out of the cafeteria, we passed my sister Josephine in her polka-dot bows surrounded by girls trying to dress just like her. She scrunched up her eyes at me and said, "Merlin, what were you thinking?"

CHAPTER 4

Bubble Gum and One Freaky Creature

Principal Williams took one look at Findlehorner holding me up by my collar and sentenced me to cleaning the cafeteria during recess. By the look on his face, I realized Principal Williams was scared of Findlehorner, too. While A'lo and all his buddies played football, and Global and all his buddies traded Pokémon cards on the playground, I scraped bubble gum off the bottoms of tables.

"Man, this has to be child abuse," I grumbled. I couldn't believe how many ill-mannered, bubble-blowing students stuck gum under the tables. My mom would have killed me if I did something like that!

I imagined those wads of gum stretched from end to end just like stars from a gumball galaxy. A galaxy is a system of millions or billions of stars, gas, and dust, held together in space by gravitational attraction. The gumball galaxy reminded me of the smartest astronomer of all time, Orbit

Gibbons. He said there was a monumental meteor shower headed this way in less than a week! Hundreds of flaming pieces of asteroids will be shooting out of the sky toward earth.

Have you ever seen him on T.V.? I mean Orbit Gibbons is like some real-life superhero with super-brain powers. Dude knows everything there is to know about space! I couldn't wait to watch those fireballs magnified by the new telescope my dad bought me for Christmas.

Big Monty versus the Fireball . . . and . . . action!"

For a minute, I forgot all about how unfair it was that A'lo was on the playground while I was stuck under a table. All Findlehorner gave me to work with was one plastic spoon. Just as I scraped at a massive wad of purple gum, the spoon snapped in half.

"Great," I said, and crawled out from under the table to go ask for another spoon. When I pushed the metal doors toward the kitchen open, I heard it. Findlehorner was talking to some dude.

"There you are, my pet," she crooned. By crooned I mean she sounded all sappy like she was talking to somebody she had the feels for. I knew that couldn't be true. That lady doesn't even have a heart, no sir, not Findlehorner.

"That's right," I heard her laugh. "Come to mama." Was it a kid? Findlehorner had a kid? No way.

I stretched as tall as I could on my toes and peeked into the round, plastic window in the swinging door. I couldn't believe what I saw.

No lie, there was Findlehorner talking to a creature that was two feet taller than her! It had a pizza for a head, moldy loaves of bread for arms and legs, a crusty pan of lasagna for a stomach and chest, and meat-loaf for hands and feet.

I jumped back and rubbed my eyes. I must have gotten lost in that bubble gum galaxy. Then, I heard Findlehorner say, "You are finally ready to teach those spoiled brats a lesson! Tomorrow's lunch will be one those kids never forget." Findlehorner laughed like some character off of Cartoon Network. I was sure I was dreaming or going crazy. And then things got worse. I heard it talk.

"Teach them a lesson," it slobbered out of its fish stick mouth, which scared me so much I stumbled through the door. I was inches from that rotting food monster, and I could smell it. That creature reeked like twenty-four camel farts mixed with spoiled milk, I swear!

Findlehorner looked deranged, like that freaky clown from the scary movie my mom won't let me watch. It spooked me so bad, I jumped up off the floor, like when Stephen Curry sunk the buzzer beater from the three-quarter court, and backed out that kitchen faster than Mentos out of a Coke bottle.

Ever tried the Mentos and Coke experiment? It looks like a geyser, which is a hot spring of water under the earth that boils and sends water shooting into the air. Really cool. Totally defies gravity, which is the force that pulls everything toward the ground. It's why we don't float around like astronauts and why people say basketball stars like Michael Jordan "defy gravity" when they jump so high. Defy means to disobey— kind of like A'lo does to Principal Williams. When something "defies gravity," it doesn't fall to the ground like it's supposed to.

What are you waiting for? Ask your mom what job she needs done around the house so she'll take you to the store this weekend to get your materials!

How to Defy Gravity

Materials

Liter bottle of Diet Coke or Pepsi
Package of Mentos candy

Directions

This experiment should be done outside in an open area.

1. Take one or two pieces of Mentos candy out of the wrapper.

2. Open the bottle of diet cola, drop a piece of candy into it, quickly step back out of the way, and watch it erupt!

To make an even bigger geyser use warm soda, and do the experiment on a warm day. Or, drop in all the candy at the same time, put your hand over the top and shake it all up. Step back quickly when you let go. BOOM!

CHAPTER 5

Coach Hamhock and One Delusional Principal

I knew there was only one person in the school tough enough to help me with this situation. Coach Hamhock was a three-time Olympic deadlift champion. She suffered from some kind of mental meltdown when she didn't meet the qualifications in her last tryouts.

Rumor had it that when she found out she'd been cut, one of the judges disappeared on a birdwatching trip. No one has seen him since. Her therapist told her she needed to share her competitive spirit with young people. That's how she came to teach P.E. at Washington Carver.

When I came into the gym, Coach Hamhock was yelling at three poor kindergarteners in push-up position who were trembling so hard that it looked like they were being electrocuted in plank pose. Their faces had a gravitational attraction to that gym floor!

"Thirty more seconds!" She screeched in her Bronx accent, which totally stuck out here in Memphis, Tennessee.

I raced up to Hamhock and told her as fast as I could, "Coach, Mrs. Findlerhorner is out of control. She's built some kind of food creature to take us out!"

"What's that? Findlehorner has a new food feature? I'm straight leans and greens. Thank you anyway."

"No! She has a food creature she wants to unleash on us ungrateful kids!"

"Ungrateful like these puny specimens who don't appreciate top-notch Olympic preparation?"

"Coach, they're kindergarteners!"

"You think they have it hard? When I was in kindergarten in the Bronx, we trained by catching sewer rats for the city. Merlin, either get down and give me thirty or get out of my gym!" I took a look at the pool of sweat forming under those kindergarteners, and I shot out there like I was trying out for the track team!

The last place I wanted to go was back to the principal's office, but this was an emergency. Mr. Williams wins the gold star principal award for the state every year. He wears three-piece suits to school every day but Friday, and his motto is Expect Excellence! Surely Mr. Williams could figure out what to do.

I flew past the secretary and pushed open the door to Principal William's office without even knocking. I couldn't believe what I saw!

There was Principal Williams behind his desk holding a selfie stick with the red, live video light flashing. He wore a throwback WWE wrestling mask over his head that looked like it was borrowed from Rey Mysterio.

He seemed to be in pain. He was grunting like a constipated pig and wiggling from side to side with his arm in a macho man position, fist curled. Under his grunts, I heard him say, "Not this time, Cold Stone. Can you smell this Spinebuster I'm about to serve you?"

What in the world was he doing? Making a YouTube video in the middle of the school day? I was so embarrassed, I threw my hands up in the air and walked out before he noticed me. Was every adult in this school insane?

CHAPTER 6

Frozen with
One Smart Sister

I'd run out of ideas. At this point, I had no faith left in anyone over three feet tall. There was only one person left who could help this situation, but I didn't want to admit who it was.

I crept down to the third-grade hall to Ms. Jackson's room and peeked in the window.

Ms. Jackson was surrounded by children with their butts glued to their seats and their eyes glued on her. In the very center sat my sister, Josephine, covered in polka dots. Polka dots were her signature style. By signature, I mean that Josephine thinks wearing them every day shows her personality. She has polka dot socks, shoes, headbands, and even fingernail polish.

I opened the door, and Ms. Jackson smiled at me, "Can I help you, Merlin?"

"Um, yes ma'am," I thought fast. "I need Josephine in the office because um, um, she won another art award."

"Another one? How wonderful," said Ms. Jackson.

Josephine popped up off the floor, glared at me, and followed me out of her classroom. In the hallway, she put her hands on her hips and said, "Merlin, what kind of dumb excuse was that? What's going on?"

"Listen, I need your help. Mrs. Findlerhorner has lost it! She's built some kind of food creature. She plans to destroy the school because no one likes her meatloaf!"

"What are you talking about? Have you been watching too many sci-fi movies?" Sci-fi is short for science fiction. Fiction means fake, or at least not real. I love using my imagination when it comes to science, but there was no scientific explanation for what I saw in that cafeteria. Findlehorner must have some kind of recipe for magic. Really? Magic? There had to be another answer.

"Come with me." I grabbed her hand and pulled her toward the cafeteria. I was running so fast her short legs could barely keep up. When I looked back, she was grinning.

"What are you so happy about?"

"You're holding my hand in school," she said.

"What? Yuck!" I dropped her hand. Josephine is one of the most confident kids

I know. She wouldn't be caught dead with a hair out of place or a pair of shoes that didn't perfectly match her outfit. For some unknown reason, I'm her favorite person on earth. It's embarrassing.

Josephine is clever. She can figure out things that nobody else can. When she was three she snagged my Popular Science magazine. Once, when she was five, the garbage disposal went crazy and spit bananas on the ceiling of the kitchen. My stepdad took the sink apart but couldn't get it back together. I went into the kitchen to get a snack and saw my baby sister under the sink, with a wrench in her hand.

Wouldn't you know it? That garbage disposal worked after that.

I needed Josephine's cleverness now. Somebody had to deal with this lunch lady situation.

We snuck down to the cafeteria. Josephine and I crawled under the tables like spies in Mission Impossible. We peeked through the slot where you slide your dirty trays into the kitchen. Josephine's eyes got big.

"What is that?"

"That? That is the last forty-five lunch leftovers served at Washington Carver." The food creature turned its pizza head towards us. One of his pepperoni eyes was slightly higher than the other. He had a carton of strawberry milk in each hand and several empty cartons surrounding him on the floor. Spoiled milk ran down the corners of his mouth and spilled all over his disgusting face.

"Ewww," said Josephine. "I just threw up in my mouth a little bit. That thing ree-aaallly likes strawberry milk! What are you going to do about that heap of hot mess?"

"That's what I was hoping you would help with."

Just then I felt a shadow come over us. I looked up, and Mrs. Findlehorner had industrial strength, metal salad tongs in each hand. I almost swallowed my tongue when that woman snapped us up with her lobster-like pinchers. She dragged us across the kitchen floor, flung us in the walk-in freezer, and slammed it shut!

Signature

What's your signature? Signature means a couple of things. An example of the first meaning of signature is like Josephine's polka dots. It's what you're known for. A'lo's signature is his fake grill. Only A'lo would have the nerve to wear something like that. Global's signature is being the smartest kid in our school. I'm not sure what mine is yet. I'm still working on it.

The second meaning of signature is your first and last name written in cursive. You put your signature on forms, documents, and checks. Problem is, schools stopped teaching cursive when I was in second grade, so I didn't learn how to do my signature. I had to learn on my own by looking up cursive on the internet and practicing. I suggest you do the same, so you don't look like a fool when some young kid asks for your autograph one day.

Big Monty

CHAPTER 7

Treasure and Hundreds of Unbelievable Rats

"What are we going to do?" Josephine shivered.

"I was counting on you!" I rattled the door of the giant walk-in freezer. No luck. I heard a whoosh sound as the thermostat kicked on and cold air blew into the freezer. The thermostat on the wall read

30 degrees Fahrenheit—two degrees below the freezing point. I knew frostbite could begin in our extremities within five minutes. Extremities are the parts of your body that stick out like your fingers, toes, and nose. We had to hurry.

"Josephine, come help me. I see a vent in the ceiling."

We stacked up bags of Chunky Chicken nuggets, frozen cheese slices, and boxes of crinkle fries to the top of the freezer. I climbed up on the teetering tower. "Whoa!" A loose bag of nuggets almost gave way, but I caught myself on a box of Mighty Meatballs.

"Look at this!" Josephine called from the floor. She held up a box that had been hidden under the nuggets. It looked like an old pirate chest out of a movie.

"Open it," I called down. "It might have something to help us get out of here." I stretched as far as I could toward the ceiling to reach a screw and unfasten the vent. The temperature was dropping. I knew we didn't have long before we would be frozen as solid as the box of creamed spinach.

Josephine creaked open the frozen lid of the mysterious box. It was full of old, yellowing newspapers. She dug through pieces of newspaper, frantically throwing them all over the place. "Nothing," she called.

I looked down. "Wait! All those newspapers have Mrs. Findlehorner's face on them!" I called from the food tower.

Just then, I heard a scratching noise above me. Josephine's head snapped up and she froze, staring at me as if she'd seen a ghost.

Very quietly, Josephine said, "Merlin. Don't. Look. Up." What do you do when someone says not to do something? Yup. I looked up.

Coming out of the grate in the vent was an enormous, scaly tail. The grate began to wiggle, and before I could get out of the way it burst open. Staring straight into my face were two icepick teeth, one pointy rodent nose, and whiskers coated with icicles. Where was Coach Hamhock when you needed her?

"Merlin, jump!"

I leaped back, and the entire food ladder crashed underneath me. Josephine and I stood huddled in terror when not one but two huge creatures shoved their freaky faces through the vent. I'd never seen an ice rat on the nature channel, but I couldn't think of any other name to call what was staring us down. Then, it got worse.

We heard scratching all above our heads like the sound of my mom's poodle, Tink, scratching at our back door, only thousands of them. Josephine and I stood trembling in front of the freezer door when, Boom! Ice rats shot out of the vent like a fire hydrant exploding.

"Move!" I screamed. Josephine dove one way. I dove the other. The herd of ice rats slammed into the freezer door with such force that the door shot open.

"Run!" Josephine screamed. We ran so fast we left our shadows behind us.

Yo, while I was trying not to freeze to death in the school cooler, I was reminded of one of the best things to do when your mother makes you babysit your younger brother or sister. I used to amuse Josephine with this one for hours.

Take a few blocks or hard plastic toys—little dinosaurs or Legos are good.

Put them in a bowl and cover them with water.

Stick them in the freezer until they become a block of ice.

Now, tell your sibling they are an archeologist—archeologists are scientists who study history by digging up old artifacts and mummies and other cool stuff. They have to dig out fossils very carefully, without breaking them. Give your brother or sister a spoon, toothpicks, and salt and tell them to get the fossils out of the ice. The salt is a cheat. It helps the ice melt faster, but it usually takes them a while to figure that out.

While they're at it, you can go play your video game in peace!

CHAPTER 8

Extra! Extra! and a World-Renowned Chef

That night, while our mom was supervising the late shift at the hospital in the neonatal unit, Josephine and I started working on a plan. By the way, neonatal means our mom takes care of newborn babies wrapped up tight like mini burritos.

I kept trying to think about how scientists say that magic is just smoke and mirrors, how magicians just make you think you are seeing something real. That Meatloaf Monster couldn't be real, could it?

Something also kept bugging me about those newspapers in the freezer. They all had pictures of Findlehorner. What had she done to make the front page so many times? With one quick internet search, Josephine figured out everything.

Josephine read the titles of several articles out loud. "Findlehorner Wins Blue Ribbon at State Fair Pie Contest."

"Local Woman to be Featured on Burnt, a National Cooking Show."

"Linda Findlehorner Wins New Cooking Show Host Position"

"Findlehorner Fired!"

"Wow!" said Josephine. "It says here she was fired because her meatloaf made the contestants sick."

"That's not a surprise," I said, as I cleaned the last of the ice rat poop off my sneakers.

"But, they later found out that her rival, Jon Le Pew, planted laxatives in her meat because he lost the competition against her."

"Really?" I said. "Are you sure we have the right woman?"

"Yes. Look at the last sentence. It says Findlehorner disappeared but is rumored to be working in a school somewhere."

Picturing Findlehorner anywhere other than behind the cafeteria line was hard, but the facts didn't lie. "Wow. Poor Mrs. Findlehorner. That's messed up to have your title taken. She was a gourmet chef!"

"That gourmet chef has flipped one too many fish sticks," Josephine said. "We have to figure out what to do with her food weapon."

Josephine tapped her polka dot fingernails while she thought. "I have an idea,"

she said. "That creature really liked strawberry milk."

It did seem to like strawberry milk as much as I did. But, Josephine found something on the internet that made me think twice about my favorite school lunch beverage— see below. Warning: do not read if you want to keep your love for pink milk.

Here's what Josephine found on the internet. "Strawberry milk doesn't actually contain strawberries. It does not come from pink cows. It does not even come from cows who ate strawberries. Strawberry milk is just milk with almost 20 grams of sugar and red dye added."

Yuck! That's like when I saw that YouTube video on how hot dogs are really made, and don't get me started on chicken nuggets. #ThingsIWishINeverLearned

CHAPTER 9

Weeble Waffles and a Showdown

The next morning, Josephine and I got to school early. We snuck around the back of Washington Carver where the food delivery trucks load and unload. We waited behind the dumpster for the food and milk truck to arrive. It smelled like fish guts and gerbil breath mixed together.

"I can't breathe," said Josephine.

"Breathe through your mouth," I told her. Finally, the food truck arrived and backed up to the cafeteria door.

"Ok Josephine, you're up."

Josephine took her short-self up to the side of that truck and plastered a big smile across her face. The driver stepped out and said, "Can I help you?"

"Did you know it's Waffle Wednesday at the Weeble Waffle just down the street?" Josephine asked the driver.

"What's that?"

"It's where they give delivery drivers all the waffles they can eat for free. But only on Wednesdays and only until 8 o'clock."

The delivery guy looked at his watch, "It's 7 forty-five!"

"You better hurry. We'll unload your boxes as part of the student volunteer team." Josephine smiled her sweetest smile. That man took off like a Lambo on Grand Theft Auto.

"Good job, Sissy!" I jumped in the back of the delivery truck. I grabbed two cartons of strawberry milk and tore them open. "It's on! Big Monty versus The Mold Monster. I'm going to challenge this bread-headed, cheese-pimpled, moldy-mouthed brute to a strawberry milk chugging duel."

I threw the cafeteria door open and yelled, "Hey, Dog Food Face! Meet me out back and chug milk like a school kid!"

I heard pots and pans banging around in the kitchen. One meatloaf hand reached out of the door. I kept my eyes on the creature as I backed into the delivery truck, luring him with the strawberry milk. He lurched and lunged after me, slobber running out of his fish stick mouth. That pile of stank followed me straight into the delivery truck.

I threw the cartons of milk toward the far corner of the truck and yelled, "Go get it, you camel-poot smellin', crusty eyebrow licking, rotten booty shaking Wasteoid!" That funky food freak lunged for his milk. I leaped out of the truck and rolled the back door down faster than Global solves a math problem. Slam! It was trapped.

Just as I clicked the lock, I heard the motor crank. "What the...?" Surely that delivery guy couldn't be back already. I ran around to the driver's side. "Wait!" I called.

But instead of the delivery guy, I saw poofy black hair and polka-dotted bows, barely peeking over the window. "Josephine, what are you doing?"

"Oh, I got this Bro!" With that, Josephine stomped on the gas, whipped that truck around the corner and over a curb.

"Josephine! You can drive?" She didn't answer me. And all I saw was dust!

CHAPTER 10

Lunch Budgets and the Real Findlehorner

Before I could recover from the sight of Josephine driving, I felt a shiver on the back of my neck, that feeling when you just know somebody's looking at you before you turn around. I could feel her beady eyes burning holes right through my freshly cut fro, just like she burns that meatloaf on Monday. Mrs. Finderhorner.

I turned around slowly and faced that long, vulture-looking nose. She looked like she was ready to pick my bones clean. Findlehorner was so angry that her normal greasy, slicked-back hair had come all undone and stuck straight out from her head like a mad Medusa. Medusa is a monster from Greek mythology with real live snakes for hair and if you look at her face, you turn to stone!

"What did you do with my darling creation?" she screeched as she moved toward me with an egg beater in one hand like she was going to whisk me into a scrambled omelet.

"Listen, Mrs. Findlehorner, I know the real deal. I know that you were a blue-ribbon baker. I know that you were such a good cook that you had your own T.V. show. And, I know that you got robbed of your reputation as one of the best cooks in America by some chump who was jealous of you."

Findlehorner froze, and her face began to soften. "If only they had believed me."

"I believe you. I know the truth." I said. "You could be a great chef again! Feeding kids nutritious food is important work."

The corners of her lips turned up, almost into a smile. For a moment even her hair seemed to relax. Her small eyes brightened with hope. Her shoulders dropped with despair, and she covered her eyes. "How am I supposed to do my job well with budget cuts? There's barely money left to keep Ms. Freddy around, and the food I'm forced to order is horrible."

She had a point. Public schools never get enough money for teachers, let alone lunch ladies.

Just then, a delivery truck rolling on two wheels shot around the corner like it was leaving a heist. I saw Josephine's poofy hair barely poking over the steering wheel. This was not the delivery truck she drove off in.

"What the...?"

In big letters on the side of the truck said, "Jon Le Pew's Fine Dining Experience—We Only Serve the Best!"

Josephine hopped down out of that truck and said, "Here you go, Mrs. Findlerhorner. I thought you could use some improved in-gredients."

CHAPTER 11

Big Monty Serves Lunch Lady Respect

The next day, I didn't worry what A'lo or anybody thought as I stood in line next to old Ms. Freddy serving half-pound gourmet ribeye steaks, grilled asparagus that gave vegetables a good name, and sweet potato á la mode. Mrs. Finderhorner really knew how to do it right with decent food.

I agreed to help Mrs. Finderhorner gain some respect from the students, as long as I got a second helping of those sweet potatoes.

"'Sup, Big Monty?" A'lo and his buddies nodded at me over their cafeteria trays. "You doin' it right with this food, Bruh."

"Good afternoon, Big Monty-Merlin," called Global, as I scooped an extra-large portion of sweet potatoes onto his plate. That big dude needs a lot of fuel to keep his brain going.

I found out Mrs. Findlehorner wasn't only good at cooking. She was good at science, too—movie science, that is. Turns out her food monster was actually a combination of cinematography, computer animation, and chemical reactions that produced the horrible stank on a hologram. A hologram is a three-dimensional image formed by the interference of light beams from a laser or other light source. Remember lasers from chapter two?

Yup. Some days are just all right.

Josephine started a custom-made hair bow club after school with all the third-grade girls to raise money for better food in the cafeteria. Those things were hot. Every girl at Washington Carver Elementary sported hair bows made out of their favorite pattern.

The kids at school began to look forward to lunch, but I heard Jon Le Pew's Fine Dining Experience wasn't so fine anymore. Rumor had it, he had started serving meatloaf.

Me? I'm just looking forward to that meteor shower this weekend. Big Monty is out. Peace.

THE END

Hey, Reader. Matt Maxx here. Want to see what chemical reaction Mrs. Findlehorner used to make the Food Monster slobber? Try this in your kitchen!

Food Monster Slobber

Materials

Ask a parent to help you find baking soda, vinegar, dish soap, and an empty water bottle. Promise them you'll clean up afterwards!

Procedure

1. Place an empty 8-12 oz water bottle on the kitchen counter.
2. Add 1 teaspoon (tsp) of baking soda and a drop of dish soap into the bottle.
3. Measure out 5 teaspoons (tsps) of vinegar into a cup.
4. Pour the cup of vinegar into the water bottle.
5. Watch the slobber flow!

What is happening?

A chemical reaction (a chemical change). These are written in form called chemical equations like this:

$$C_2H_4O_2 + NaHCO_3 \rightarrow NaC_2H_3O_2 + H_2O + CO_2$$

Acetic Acid +	Sodium =	Sodium	+ Water +	Carbon
	Bicarbonate	Acetate		Dioxide

The combination of the vinegar (acetic acid) with baking soda (sodium bicarbonate) yield or makes sodium acetate, water, and carbon dioxide (gas). The soap makes the reaction easier to see but it doesn't do anything else. The formation of a gas is a sign that a chemical change has occurred.

CPSIA information can be obtained
at www.ICGtesting.com
Printed in the USA
BVHW070901020520
579075BV00005B/1330

9 781733 743501